SCHOOL DAYS

SCHOOL DAYS

By B.G. Hennessy

Pictures by Tracey Campbell Pearson

Puffin Books

Special thanks to the teachers and children
of Jericho Elementary and Heathcote School.

T.C.P. and B.G.H.

The artwork for each painting consists of an ink,
watercolor, and gouache painting that was camera
separated and reproduced in full color.

PUFFIN BOOKS
Published by the Penguin Group
Penguin Books USA Inc., 375 Hudson Street, New York, New York 10014, U.S.A.
Penguin Books Ltd, 27 Wrights Lane, London W8 5TZ, England
Penguin Books Australia Ltd, Ringwood, Victoria, Australia
Penguin Books Canada Ltd, 10 Alcorn Avenue, Toronto, Ontario, Canada M4V 3B2
Penguin Books (N.Z.) Ltd, 182–190 Wairau Road, Auckland 10, New Zealand

Penguin Books Ltd, Registered Offices: Harmondsworth, Middlesex, England

First published in the United States of America by Viking Penguin,
a division of Penguin Books USA Inc., 1990
Published in Puffin Books, 1992

10 9 8

Text copyright © B.G. Hennessy, 1990
Illustrations copyright © Tracey Campbell Pearson, 1990
All rights reserved

LIBRARY OF CONGRESS CATALOGING-IN-PUBLICATION DATA
Hennessy, B. G. (Barbara G.)
     School days / by B.G. Hennessy; pictures by Tracey Campbell Pearson.   p. cm.
     Summary: Rhyming text and illustrations describe the familiar
faces and objects of a day at school.
     ISBN 0-14-054179-9
     [1. Schools—Fiction.   2. Stories in rhyme.]   I. Pearson, Tracey Campbell, ill.   II. Title.
[PZ8.3.H418Sc   1992]   [E]—dc20   92-12008

Printed in the United States of America

For all the
teachers
who make
school fun

B.G.H. and T.C.P.

School bus, cubby, starting bell

Circle time, then show and tell.

Bookshelves, desks, pencil sharpener,

New friends, old friends, plant monitor.

Shapes and numbers, alphabet,
Puzzles, blocks, classroom pet.

Making rhymes and letter games,
Telling time and learning names.

Matthew, Dee, Mark and Claire,
Jason, Nancy and Pierre.

Molly, Sam and Gregory,
Ruby, Max and Hillary.

Daniel, Jill and Jennifer,
Gail, Rebecca, Christopher.

MS. GREEN'S
CLASS

ROOM 6

Crayons, scissors, markers, glue,

Smocks and paper, a perfect blue.

Music teacher, Librarian,

Coach and Nurse, Custodian.

Lunch box, sandwich, popcorn, juice,

Cookies, apple, Matt's front tooth!

Recess, fun time, run, jump, race,
Ball and tag, touch home base.

Feeling sad, feeling mad,
Someone has been very bad.

Seesaw, swings and sky high slides,

One more minute, one last ride.

Hearing stories, sitting still,

Listen, line up, fire drill!

Writing, reading, practicing,

Waiting for the bell to ring.

Backpack, work book, pencil case,

Everything is in its place.

Now it's time for school to end
Say goodbye to all your friends.